GW00854460

The Dia

Robin's Travels

Sweet Cherry
Publishing

Published by Sweet Cherry Publishing Limited
Unit E, Vulcan Business Complex
Vulcan Road
Leicester, LE5 3EB
United Kingdom

www.sweetcherrypublishing.com

First published in the UK in 2016
ISBN: 978-1-78226-251-0
© Ken Lake 2016
Illustrations © Creative Books
Illustrated by Vishnu Madhav

The Diaries of Robin's Travels: Las Vegas

Printed and Bound in India
I.TP002

Las Vegas

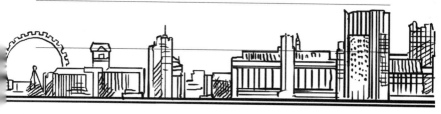

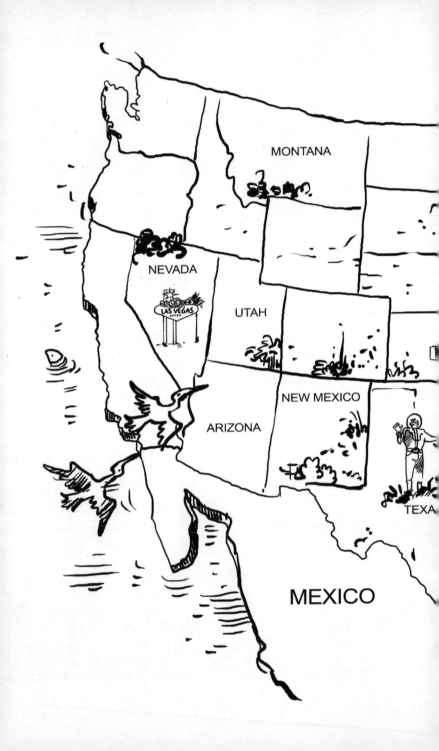

It was Saturday morning. Robin was eating his breakfast and sitting by the window. He was thinking about doing his homework, but he wanted to ask Grandad if he could borrow his map first.

It was a quiet morning and not much was going on outside. The only thing Robin could see in the street was Mrs Brown's cat, Tiddles, who was trotting along the fence.

Such a good sense of balance! Robin thought to himself.

Then Tiddles stopped, shuffled his feet, and hopped up into the tree.

"Tiddles, where are you?" Mrs Brown poked her head out of the front door.

She looked up and saw her cat sat up in the tree. He meowed loudly and sheepishly looked at his owner.

"Oh Tiddles, you silly thing!" Mrs Brown hurried

outside. "I can't possibly call the fire brigade

again. I'll come and get you myself this time!"

With that, Mrs Brown grabbed her stepladder

and propped it up next to the tree.

10

She climbed up a few branches and reached out to grab Tiddles. But Tiddles had other ideas: he bounced down a few branches and landed perfectly with his four furry paws on the ground.

"Oh bother," said Mrs Brown. She looked down at Tiddles, then back up at the branches.

"Mum!" Robin called. "Come quickly, Mum!"

Mum came hurrying into the living room and frowned at Robin.

"What's going on this time? Is Tiddles stuck up Mrs Brown's tree again?" she asked with a chuckle.

"No!" Robin said, "*Mrs Brown* is stuck up Mrs Brown's tree."

Mum and Robin both rushed outside.

"Don't worry, Mrs Brown!" Robin called up to her.

"We're going to get help!" Mum said.

So that is what they did.

The fire brigade soon arrived with its blue lights flashing and bells ringing.

"Well, Mrs Brown. I am shocked!" said the fire chief as he carried her down the ladder. "I expected to find Tiddles up there, but not you!"

Mrs Brown was a little bit shaken up. She brushed herself down and scowled at Tiddles.

After the commotion was over, Robin and Mum went inside.

Ring, ring, ring, ring!

Robin grabbed the phone.

"Hello, Robin!" Grandad said.

"Hello, Grandad!" Robin said. "You will never guess what just happened," Robin told Grandad all about Mrs Brown getting stuck in the tree.

"Oh dear," Grandad chuckled. "But how was your week at school?"

"It was great, Grandad. My history and geography marks just keep getting better!" Robin said. "I have some homework to do though, and I was hoping that you might be able to help me."

"I will try, Robin."

Robin told Grandad all about his geography homework, which was to label a map of the **USA**.

"I have to write the names of the different states on my map."

"That's a lot of states to think of! There are 50 altogether," said Grandad.

Grandad told Robin he would bring over his world map for him to use.

"That's great. Thanks, Grandad."

"In fact, I think another trip might be in order, to say well done for your good marks," he replied.

"That would be amazing, Grandad. I do have some holidays soon," Robin grinned. He felt excited already.

"Yes, and Mum and Grandma are going on their hiking trip to Wales next week too."

"Perfect timing!" Robin said. "Where will we be going?"

"Well I think we should take a trip over to the USA," Grandad said.

"Wow! Really?" Robin jumped up and down and almost dropped the phone.

"Yes, Robin!" Grandad chuckled. "We'll go as soon as your school holiday starts. Remember . . ."

"Passport, visa and camera," Robin said quickly and laughed.

"Well done, you're learning!"

Grandad asked Robin to pass the phone to Mum so that he could arrange their trip.

The next week went slowly for Robin. He knew it was because he was excited and couldn't wait for his trip with Grandad. He was going to the United States of America!

When the weekend finally came, he sat by the front door with his suitcase, camera and passport.

Beep, beep, beep, beep!

Robin grabbed his stuff, gave Mum a big hug, and ran down the garden path to the little red car.

When they got on the plane, Grandad brought

out some sweets and his notepad.

"It's going to be a long journey, Robin," he

said, sucking on a humbug.

"Well, Grandad, I don't even know where

we're going!" Robin folded his arms and frowned

at Grandad.

"Ah, of course," Grandad chuckled. "We'll be going to **Nevada**, which is a state in the south west of America. We'll be flying over the **Atlantic Ocean**, so make sure you have a look out of your window."

22

"I don't think I've ever heard anything about Nevada," said Robin, scratching his head.

"Well, it's mostly famous for a city that calls itself the entertainment capital of the world."

Robin smiled.

"Now, I think I know where that is!" he said.

"You do?" said Grandad .

"Las Vegas!"

They both laughed.

"It has the biggest population in the whole state, with over half a million people."

"Do they use the **American dollar?**" Robin asked.

"Of course," Grandad showed him a dollar note and all the coins he had prepared for their trip.

"What are the coins? Are they **nickels**?" Robin picked one of the coins up.

"Yes, exactly! They also have **dimes**, **cents** and **quarters**." Grandad picked each coin up one by one. "You see, a dollar is worth one hundred cents. A nickel is five cents, a dime is ten cents, and a quarter is twenty five cents."

"But what about **bucks**, Grandad?" Robin asked.

"A buck is slang for a dollar."

Grandad put the coins away. He then pulled out a smaller version of his world map and showed Robin where they would be going.

The flight was twelve hours long! Grandad spent most of it asleep, but Robin only slept for a little bit. He was happy to look at the map and watch the clouds rolling by the window.

Once they landed, they hopped in a taxi that took them to the centre of the city.

Las Vegas was busy and so sunny! Even in the daytime, Robin could see the bright lights and **neon** signs.

"This is amazing," Robin said, his eyes were

wide with excitement.

"Now, I think we must be on **Las Vegas**

Boulevard, although it's better known as **the**

Strip." Grandad took out his map, and they began to walk down the long road.

All around them were tall buildings and hotels. Each one was bigger than the next!

Robin saw a small version of the **Eiffel Tower**. He grabbed Grandad's arm.

"Look!" he pointed to the tower. "We saw the real one in **Paris**, but I didn't expect to see one here."

Robin and Grandad decided that they would go to the hotel first and catch up on some sleep. After that they could start their adventure. They were still very tired from their journey, and they didn't want **jet lag**, after all!

Their hotel was very big and had been made to look like a castle.

Robin loved it. He felt like a knight from an old story. The inside was brightly coloured and full of people. There were funfair games, and he could see the swimming pool through the back doors.

"So, what do you think?" Grandad grinned.

Robin didn't know what to say. He smiled at Grandad and shook his head, he couldn't believe it!

Once they had slept, they went out onto the Strip. It was very crowded. Robin took a few photos, but it was difficult with so many people!

"Wow, Grandad, it's so busy," said Robin.

"Let's go out of the centre for a bit," Grandad pulled out his map. "I know of a few good places that you might like."

They took a taxi to the outskirts of the city.

Grandad took the little magical book from his

pocket and looked at Robin.

Robin grinned. He was very excited.

Grandad cast the spell.

Little book, make it so,

Tell us all we need to know.

People, places, countries, towns,

Show the jewels in all these crowns!

Then something wonderful happened. The book flipped open to a picture of vast desert. Then it began to shake and sparkling dust burst from the pages. Suddenly, from out of this glittering cloud, there appeared a Native American woman no bigger than Grandad's finger. She was wearing a long brown dress, with beads around her neck and in her long dark hair. She stretched and yawned before finally speaking to them.

"Hello! Thank you for waking me up. Who are you?"

"I'm Robin, and this is Grandad," said Robin,

"but . . . who are you?"

"My name is **Sarah Winnemucca [win-eh-moo-ka]**," she smiled. "I was part of the **Paiute [pie-oot]** tribe. Our tribe were the native inhabitants of Nevada."

"So you lived here, Sarah?" Robin asked.

She smiled and nodded, "Yes, before there were any big cities, and when the land was all desert and springs."

The taxi stopped by a group of wooden shacks that seemed to be abandoned. They got out. Robin got dust all over his shoes very quickly!

"This desert is called the **Mojave [mo-har-vey] Desert**," Sarah pointed all around them.

It was very hot. Grandad began to fan himself with his notepad, and Robin put his hat on.

"It's really hot!" Robin said. "But it doesn't look much like a desert: there are lots of bushes."

He and Grandad put on their sunglasses and suncream then looked around. Robin clicked his camera at a cactus and the wild grasses.

"Well, do you know what 'Las Vegas' means?" Sarah asked.

"Erm . . ." Robin looked at Grandad, who shrugged. "No, I don't think so."

"It is Spanish for 'The Meadows'," their little guide smiled and held her arm out to the landscape. "When the Spanish settlers arrived in the 1820s, they were surprised by the wild grasses and desert spring waters. They thought

it looked like a meadow, even if it was boiling hot

out here!"

"Where did you live in the desert, Sarah? It

must have been hard for you." Robin asked.

"We lived in an area known as the **Wetlands**.

You're right, the weather and land can be harsh

around here. We made sure that we stayed

where there was fresh water and fish for us to

eat," she replied, "but there were other Paiute tribes all over this desert, in the north and south, and the east and west too."

"Wow!" Robin said. "Did they live on the wetlands too?"

Sarah nodded.

Grandad started to scribble down some notes.

"When I was a young girl, little towns like this were the only ones that existed," Sarah led them to the wooden shacks close by. "My tribe did not live in buildings like these, though."

Robin looked around. All of the little huts and cabins were dusty and falling down. One bigger building had a sign that said **Saloon** above the

door and there was another one that said Jail.

It made him think of the old cowboy films he liked

to watch with his friends.

"It's a bit spooky," Robin shuddered.

"Well this place is actually a ghost town, it used to be a town where gold miners lived," Sarah giggled. "I don't think there are really any ghosts here though, in case you were worried!"

"Thank goodness for that," said Grandad. He jumped when a light breeze made the shutters on the houses flap loudly.

42

"Gold miners?" Robin smiled. "Did they find gold here?"

"Yes, a lot of gold and silver was discovered in Nevada around the 1870s. In fact, there are many gold mines still used here. Nevada produces 79% of all the gold in America!" Sarah explained.

"Wow," Robin was looking at the desert in a different way now. He was thinking about all the gold that might be under their feet! It helped him stop thinking about the ghosts that might be hiding in the huts too.

"But I want to take you to an even more beautiful place now," Sarah said.

They hopped back into a taxi.

"Are we going on a plane?" Robin asked

excitedly, he could see planes and helicopters in

the distance.

"Actually, we're going in a helicopter!"

Robin felt very excited when he saw the

helicopter. They clambered inside and put on the

seat belts. He grinned at Sarah and Grandad as the engine roared into life and they rose into the air.

"What sort of place did you live in then, Sarah, if you didn't live in little towns like the one we just saw?" Robin asked.

"Our homes were made of large dome shaped shelters that we called **wickiups**," Sarah smiled, and made a triangle shape with her hands. "We used tree bark, sticks and straw to make them. They are cool in the summer, and warm in the winter."

Grandad continued to make notes, and Robin looked out of the helicopter window.

"We will soon cross over from Nevada and into the state of **Arizona**," she said. "This beautiful place is so big it passes over two states!" Sarah chuckled and pointed out of the window.

Robin looked out and saw a sign below them.

"**Grand Canyon National Park**," his eyes went wide and he grinned at Grandad, "we're going to see the Grand Canyon! Cool!"

Soon enough, they found themselves flying over rocky cliffs and mountains, as well as trees and deep valleys. It was beautiful!

"This is amazing!" Robin said.

"Look!" Sarah pointed. "Do you see it?"

They were hovering over a huge bridge that went across a deep rocky valley. Sarah told them it was called the **Hoover Dam Bypass Bridge**.

They looked at where she was pointing.

"And that is the Hoover Dam! It is named after **President Herbert Hoover.**"

Robin quickly took a photo and let out a low whistle. He couldn't believe the size of it! It was a huge concrete structure that filled the entire V-shape of the valley they were crossing.

"Well, it doesn't look like a hoover to me!" Grandad chuckled and winked at Robin.

"What's a hoover?" Sarah frowned and looked at Grandad.

Robin giggled and explained Grandad's silly joke to Sarah. She frowned at Grandad.

"It was built between 1931 and 1936 to stop flooding, to give water to locals, and to produce **hydroelectricity**. The lake behind it is called **Lake Mead**."

"Wait, what's hydro . . . hydrel . . . ?" Robin frowned at Sarah.

"Hydroelectricity?" Sarah said. "It's when flowing water is used to make electricity."

"Oh, I see," said Robin. "That must be good for the environment."

Then, the helicopter hovered for a moment over the canyon. The pilot told them to take a look out of the window.

"Oh dear," Grandad said as they looked over.

It was a long way down!

"Don't look down, Grandad!" Robin laughed.

It was as if Robin could see the whole state of Arizona on one side and Nevada on the other, right before his very eyes!

The canyon was very deep. There was grey and orange rock all around and in lots of different shapes. It stretched out for miles all around them.

The helicopter flew a little further, then landed on a helipad. The pilot told them they would have some time to explore.

"Where are we, Sarah?"

"We're in Arizona now," Sarah explained, "that means 'dry lands' in Spanish." She smiled, "A lots of this territory is part of the **Hualapai [Wa-la-pie] Indian Reservation**. The Hualapai tribe still live here."

"They live here?" Robin was shocked. "I don't know how you could live on these mountains!"

"Well the Hualapai tribe have always been here. They are very used to it," Sarah chuckled. "They consider the Grand Canyon to be sacred ground."

As they were about to head back to the helicopter, Robin chose a couple of little rocks and popped them into his pocket.

They flew back over the Grand Canyon and landed in Las Vegas.

"Now, before I go back into the book. I want to show you something exciting!" Sarah grinned and pointed out where to go as they hopped out of the helicopter. They were heading back towards

the Strip.

 Robin couldn't believe his eyes when he saw

it! A huge replica of a volcano erupted as they

stood and watched from the street.

"No-one will believe this back at school!" Robin said. He took a picture.

"And one more thing . . ." Sarah said, "do you like pirates, Robin?" She smiled and folded her arms. Robin thought she might know the answer already.

"Of course!" he said, "you know, I did a treasure hunt on my last birthday." He folded his arms too and gave Sarah a proud smile.

"Then follow me!" she said.

They started to hurry through the streets. Sarah was a brilliant guide! She was just as excited as they were. Soon they reached a hotel with a pool of water outside of it.

A huge pirate ship sailed out of a little bay. The pirates cried 'Ahoy!' and started attacking each other with their swords, some pirates even fell into the water.

Sarah decided it was time for her to go back into the book. Grandad and Robin thought it would be best to have a nice dinner and settle in for the night. It had been such a long day!

They found a place to have dinner before they settled down to bed. It was the strangest place Robin had ever eaten in. It looked just like a jungle. It even sounded like a jungle! There were leaves and branches stretching all over the ceiling.

Next to their table there was a huge model of an elephant. Behind other tables, there were lots of other model animals and big fish tanks.

Grandad and Robin both had huge meals and laughed a lot at everything they could see.

"Well we'd better get back to the castle . . . I mean, *hotel*!" Grandad chuckled. "I'm so tired from our long day."

So that is what they did.

The next morning was still hot and sunny. Grandad and Robin quickly got dressed and went to find somewhere to have breakfast. Sarah popped out of the little book and joined them. She struggled to drink her orange juice out of the big glass. The waiter laughed and gave her a straw.

"Where shall we go today, Sarah?" Robin asked between mouthfuls of his breakfast.

"I suggest we explore this busy city." Their little guide scratched her head, "What do you think, Grandad?"

Grandad picked a place that he thought they would all like, and they started to walk down the long road.

They walked past the collection of huge buildings, hotels and attractions. Finally, they went into a hotel that was so big on the inside that Robin didn't know what to look at first. There were people hurrying here and there with suitcases and cameras. Chandeliers hung from the ceilings, and columns of marble stood next to the huge wooden staircase.

Then, as if it couldn't get any better, there was a huge fish tank behind the front desk.

"I've never seen such a big fish tank!" said Robin said and took a photo with his camera.

"These are salt water fish!" Sarah said, "There are four hundred and fifty fish here of around eighty five different species." She grinned and looked at Robin.

"How do you know so much stuff, Sarah? I thought the city wasn't here when you were young?" Robin asked.

"I'm a tour guide, remember?" she said. "I've been here quite a few times now."

They followed signs for the gardens of this hotel.

"Wow, Grandad. What are we going to see here?" Robin said.

"Let's go and find out!"

They were all excited.

They walked through an archway with stone lions and tigers on top of it. Their stone tails dangled just above their heads!

Robin got his camera ready.

"This is a home for rare and endangered big cats and dolphins," explained Sarah said.

"**Conservationists** work very hard to keep them all safe."

In big, bright green enclosures they saw **snow tigers** and **white lions**. Robin took a photo of two little cubs as they playfully batted each other with their paws. They also saw tigers and leopards with their stripes and spots. They roared and growled at each other.

Next, they went into the dolphin section. A group of **bottlenose dolphins** were clicking and splashing in a pool in front of them.

"They are such beautiful animals!" Sarah said,

and she laughed as water splashed all over them.

Robin took a few more photos. "Mum will love

these!" he said.

Then they carried on walking and looked at all

of the other sights. There were lots of other

tourists in groups with their cameras and people

applying sun cream. Robin and Grandad were both feeling rather hot and tired from walking in the sun.

Sarah pointed out a little **Statue of Liberty**, and then she took them to see a hotel that was built like **Venice** on the inside.

"Look, there are even **gondolas [gon-doh-las]** on little canals!" Robin pointed. "We've been on one of those before."

It was nice and cool inside the hotel, and after

wandering around for a bit, Grandad and Robin

felt ready to go back outside.

Soon they passed a building with huge fountains

that seemed to dance before their eyes. They

70

splashed this way and that and reached high up into the air. Robin and Grandad stood and watched for a while.

"I wish the buildings at home could be as exciting as the ones here!" said Robin with a sigh.

"Now, you can't come to Las Vegas without getting a picture next to the **city sign**." Sarah said.

They all took a walk to the outskirts of the city, and Sarah managed to hold up the camera to take a photo of Grandad and Robin under the sign.

It was nearly night-time now, and the sign was glowing with bright bulbs and neon lights. It was red, blue and yellow and said 'Welcome to Fabulous Las Vegas!'

Sarah then took them back onto the Strip, and showed them an old wooden hut. It was surrounded by fences and had tall towers on the corners.

"This is the fort that belonged to the first settlers of Las Vegas," she told them. "It is a **Mormon fort**. Mormons are a religious group. They built this in 1855 so that they would have a place to trade and gather supplies. It's very different from what's here now, isn't it?"

"It's really different!" Robin said. "Were they the first people here?"

"No, Robin. The native tribes had been here a long time before that," Sarah smiled. "But the Mormons were the first people outside of Nevada to settle down and build here."

Robin nodded and Grandad took some notes.

"The Mormons came from **Salt Lake City, Utah [yoo - tar]**. Spanish explorers had come to Nevada before, but they didn't settle and build

anything until a few years after the Mormons."

"Did the Mormons carry on building here?"

Robin asked.

"No, they soon left this site. A lot of what

you see here is reconstructed," Sarah pointed

to different parts of the fort. "Soon, a railroad

was built through Nevada. Las Vegas first

became a city in 1905 when land next to the rail tracks was bought, and people began to build."

"So, because there was a railroad, more people could get here?" Robin asked.

He took a picture of the fort.

"That's right. It meant more people could get to the gold mines." Sarah nodded. "And then a road was built in 1926 - it is the most famous road in North America, sometimes they call it the 'Mother Road', but most people know it as **Route 66**."

Grandad smiled, "Oh yes, I know Route 66! There are lots of old songs about it!"

"Yes, exactly. Do you know, it's nearly two and a half thousand miles long?"

Sarah, Grandad and Robin looked at each other.

"That's longer than the whole of Great Britain!" Grandad shook his head.

"But Sarah, when people began to build here, what did your tribe do?" Robin asked.

"We were okay Robin, we still lived on these lands," Sarah smiled. "Sometimes people got angry and there was fighting between miners, settlers and my tribespeople."

"What did you do?" Robin asked.

"Well, my sisters and I moved away from the fighting. I married a nice young man and travelled with him through the states. I gave lectures to people about my tribe and other tribes in the country. I think it helped to show how we could all live together in one place," Sarah smiled.

"That's very brave," Robin nodded.

Sarah grinned and put her hands on her hips.

"Did you know, they called me **Paiute Princess**?"

"No!" Robin said, "I didn't know we were travelling with a princess!" His mouth fell open wide.

"I'm not really a princess," she chuckled.

"Quickly, Grandad," Robin handed Grandad his camera, "take a picture of me with a princess."

They all laughed, and Robin got a picture with Sarah.

Then they went back to the hotel and said

goodbye to Sarah. Robin gave her a little bow.

"Goodbye, Princess Sarah," he said.

Sarah grinned and hopped back into the book.

"Well, Robin, I think it's time to get some sleep.
We have to head home tomorrow!" Grandad
yawned and stretched.

They hopped into their beds.

When they got home, Mum and Grandma were
unpacking from their hiking trip in Wales.

"How was Las Vegas?" Mum asked.

"It was amazing!" Robin said. "How was your trip?"

"It was wonderful, thanks," said Mum. "I bought

you both a stick of rock!"

Mum gave Grandad and Robin stripy sticks that

smelt of mint.

Robin then put his hand in his pocket and pulled out the rocks he had picked up at the Grand Canyon. He handed one to Mum and one to Grandma.

"Well I didn't get you a stick of rock, but I did get you sacred stones, all the way from the Grand Canyon!" Robin smiled and winked at Grandad.

Want to know what Grandad's been scribbling in his notebook? Take another read through the book and note all the words in **bold** - you'll find out a little bit more about them!

Grandad's Notebook

USA: The United States of America. This is the collective name given to the fifty states, one federal district and five territories that make up the country.

Nevada: A state in the south west of the USA.

Atlantic Ocean: The second largest ocean in the world. It is bordered by North and South America in the west and Europe in the east.

Las Vegas: The most populous city of the state of Nevada, it is based in Las Vegas Valley.

American dollar: Official currency of the USA.

nickel: An American coin worth five cents.

dime: An American coin worth ten cents.

cent: A coin worth one hundredth of a dollar.

quarter: A coin that is worth twenty five cents.

bucks: An informal term for the American currency.

neon: Often used in signs. It produces a reddish, orange light, though other colours can be created.

Las Vegas Boulevard: A major road running through Las Vegas Valley.

The Strip: The portion of Las Vegas Boulevard that runs through Las Vegas.

Eiffel Tower: An iron lattice tower in Paris, France.

Paris: The capital city of France.

jet lag: A condition that occurs when people travel between time zones.

Sarah Winnemucca: A member of the Paitue tribe, based in Nevada. She was born in 1844 and was very influential in creating policies about Native American tribes in the United States. She was the first Native American woman to write an autobiography.

Paiute: A group of Native Americans made up of three bands: Northern Paiute, Owens Valley Paiute and Southern Paiute.

Mojave Desert: The desert that spreads across California, southern Nevada, south-western Utah and north-western Arizona.

Wetlands: An area that is saturated with water either permanently or seasonally.

saloon: An establishment particular to the 'Old West' or 'Wild West' where people could go for food, drink and lodging.

wickiup: A domed shelter made from curved wooden arches, tree bark and other natural materials, and used by Native American tribes in the south west of the USA.

Arizona: A state in the south west of North America.

Grand Canyon National Park: A National Park that contains the Grand Canyon, which is a gorge of the Colorado River.

Hoover Dam Bypass Bridge: The huge concrete bridge just in front of the Hoover Dam.

Hoover Dam: A concrete dam in the Black Canyon section of the Grand Canyon.

President Herbert Hoover: The thirty first President of the USA, in office from 1929 to 1933.

Lake Mead: A huge lake, or reservoir, formed by the Hoover Dam.

hydroelectricity: Electricity created by the force of falling or flowing water.

Hualapai Indian Reservation: The home of the Hualapai tribe, located in north-western Arizona.

snow tigers: Also called a White Tiger. It is a relation of the orange Bengal Tiger.

white lion: A member of the lion family are believed

to be related to African Lions.

bottlenose dolphins: A family of oceanic dolphins.

Statue of Liberty: A huge, green sculpture located on Liberty Island, New York.

Venice: A city in the north of Italy.

gondola: A flat-bottomed rowing boat that is a traditional means of transport in Venice.

city sign: A sign welcoming people to the city.

Mormon Fort: Located in downtown Las Vegas, the Mormon Fort is a reconstructed building showing the home of the first settlers of Las Vegas and Nevada.

Salt Lake City, Utah: The most populous city of the state of Utah, to the west of the USA.

Route 66: The most famous road in America, it is two thousand, four hundred and forty four (2,448) miles long.

Paiute Princess: The name often given to Sarah Winnemucca.